No Pests Allowed!

adapted by Jodie Shepherd
based on the screenplay "What's Bugging You?" by Adam Peltzman
illustrated by The Artifact Group

Ready-to-Read

SIMON SPOTLIGHT/NICKELODEON
New York   London   Toronto   Sydney

Based on the TV series *Nick Jr. The Backyardigans*™ as seen on Nick Jr.®

SIMON SPOTLIGHT
An imprint of Simon & Schuster Children's Publishing Division
1230 Avenue of the Americas, New York, New York 10020
© 2009 Viacom International Inc. All rights reserved.
NICK JR., *Nick Jr. The Backyardigans*, and all related titles, logos, and characters are trademarks
of Viacom International Inc. NELVANA™ Nelvana Limited. CORUS™ Corus Entertainment Inc.
All rights reserved, including the right of reproduction in whole or in part in any form.
SIMON SPOTLIGHT, READY-TO-READ, and colophon
are registered trademarks of Simon & Schuster, Inc.
Manufactured in the United States of America
4 6 8 10 9 7 5 3
Library of Congress Cataloging-in-Publication Data
Shepherd, Jodie.
No pests allowed!/adapted by Jodie Shepherd ; adapted from the episode
"What's Bugging You?" by Adam Peltzman. —1st ed.
p. cm. —(Ready-to-read)
"Based on the TV series Nick Jr. The Backyardigans(tm) as seen on Nick Jr.(r)."
I. Peltzman, Adam. II. Backyardigans (Television program) III. Title.
PZ7.S54373No 2009
[E]—dc22
2008017662
ISBN: 978-1-4169-7192-4
0710 LAK

Buzz! A  whizzes by.
FLY

"Buzz!"  buzzes back.
UNIQUA

"I speak ."
FLY

She flaps her arms.

"I speak  too!" says .

FLY   TYRONE

"We are from

Best Pest Control.

We know pests,

and pests know us!"

"There is a pest problem

at the  of Lady ,"

HOUSE   TASHA

says  .

UNIQUA

"We can help!"

The  opens at Lady 's .

DOOR   TASHA   HOUSE

"Hurry, hurry!" cries.

TASHA

" will be here soon!"

MR. SPIFFY

"Who is  ?" asks  .

MR. SPIFFY   UNIQUA

"He is the head of

the Spiffy Club,"  replies.

TASHA

"I want to join the club,

so my  must be spiffy."

HOUSE

"But there is a pest in my ,"
HOUSE

says . "Can you help?"
TASHA

"No problem," TYRONE tells her.

"We can help."

"Meep?" squeaks a  pest.
PURPLE

It crawls on the clean .
RUG

"Wow," says .
UNIQUA

"A  !"
WORMAN

"  are rare," says .
WORMANS   TYRONE

The  scoots away

WORMAN

and bumps into a big ⏰ .

CLOCK

Whoops! Not spiffy.

There is a knock at the .
DOOR

Oh, no! is here!
MR. SPIFFY

"Get rid of that !"
WORMAN

 tells Best Pest Control.
TASHA

"Hello, ," says  .

MR. SPIFFY   TASHA

"Welcome to my 🏠 .

HOUSE

It is very clean and neat."

"Mmm-hmm," says  .

MR. SPIFFY

"I will inspect your

HOUSE

in a jiffy. We will see."

He puts on his  .

GLOVES

"I do not like dirt or grime

or on the floor,"
SOCKS

 says.
MR. SPIFFY

"And I do not like pests!"

A  **WORMAN** wiggles behind  **MR. SPIFFY** .

Meep!  **UNIQUA** and  **TYRONE** run after it.

"Come and see the rest

of the  **HOUSE** ,"  **TASHA** says.

"Pests love snacks," says .

TYRONE

"We can make ,"  says.

CUPCAKES   UNIQUA

Mix. Pour. Spill. Whoops!

"Uh-oh," says .

TYRONE

"What a mess!"

and come in.

TASHA   MR. SPIFFY

"Oh, no!" cries . "Not spiffy!"

TASHA

She leads out of the room.

MR. SPIFFY

The 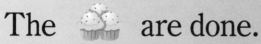 are done.
CUPCAKES

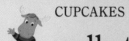 calls the .
TYRONE   WORMAN

But when he opens the ,
DOOR

many scoot in.
WORMANS

Meep! Meep! Meep!

 are everywhere!
WORMANS

The make the bouncy.
CUPCAKES   WORMANS

 bounce everywhere!
WORMANS

The  bounce on the .
WORMANS   BED

The bounce on the .
WORMANS   DRESSER

A bounces on 's head.
WORMAN   MR. SPIFFY

"What is on my head?" asks .

MR. SPIFFY

"Your ," answers .

HAT   TASHA

 catches the  in a  .

TYRONE   WORMANS   VASE

checks out the living room.

It's not spiffy at all!

There are more .

WORMANS

They are having a party.

"What a mess!" cries 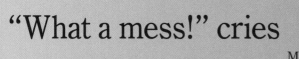 .

MR. SPIFFY

"This is not spiffy!"

Meep! Meep!

The  like to clean up.

WORMANS

They can help!

Soon the  is spiffy.
HOUSE

 is impressed.
MR. SPIFFY

"Hooray for Lady !
TASHA

Welcome to the Spiffy Club!"

Everyone has a 🧁 to celebrate.
CUPCAKE